When Santa Came to Stay

To Barnaby, with love
T. K.

For three little cheeky elves,
Tarn, Tilly and Travis
C. C.

SANTA
STOP HERE

First published in 2016
by Scholastic Children's Books
Euston House, 24 Eversholt Street London NW1 1DB
a division of Scholastic Ltd
www.scholastic.co.uk
London ~ New York ~ Toronto ~ Sydney ~ Auckland
Mexico City ~ New Delhi ~ Hong Kong

Text copyright © 2016 Timothy Knapman

Illustrations copyright © 2016 Chris Chatterton

ISBN 978 1407 16634 6

When Santa Came to Stay

Timothy Knapman ❄ Chris Chatterton

"Please let Santa stay!"
    we begged Mum and Dad.
"We promise he won't
    make a mess!"

"We've had the house painted,
    we've **dusted** and **cleaned**,"
They grumbled... "but –
        oh, all right – **yes**."

"A mess? My dear people!" said Santa. "Oh **no**,
I'm the tidiest man you could meet!
Though I may have run over a garden or two
As I landed my sleigh in your street."

We tried not to laugh!
Mum and Dad looked concerned
As they tucked us both in for the night.

Then Santa, who'd climbed into Mum and Dad's bed,
Said, "**Sweet dreams!**" and switched off the light!

"And now that is done,
    I will take you along
On my **magical**
        Christmas Eve ride."

He looked down at us
        and declared, "If you like,
You can sit at the **front**,
        by my side."

Which is how, wrapped up warm,
we flew through the sky
Next to **Santa** himself on his sleigh.

We helped him bring presents
and all of the joy
That makes Christmas
my favourite day.

"Thank you so much," our Mum and Dad said,
"For that **wonderful** treat, Santa dear."
"It was rather fun," said Santa, "and so..."

"I'll come back and stay here **NEXT** year!"